I'm Going To READ!™

These levels are meant only as guides;
you and your child can best choose a book that's right.

Level 1: Kindergarten–Grade 1 . . . Ages 4–6

- word bank to highlight new words
- consistent placement of text to promote readability
- easy words and phrases
- simple sentences build to make simple stories
- art and design help new readers decode text

Level 2: Grade 1 . . . Ages 6–7

- word bank to highlight new words
- rhyming texts introduced
- more difficult words, but vocabulary is still limited
- longer sentences and longer stories
- designed for easy readability

Level 3: Grade 2 . . . Ages 7–8

- richer vocabulary of up to 200 different words
- varied sentence structure
- high-interest stories with longer plots
- designed to promote independent reading

Level 4: Grades 3 and up . . . Ages 8 and up

- richer vocabulary of more than 300 different words
- short chapters, multiple stories, or poems
- more complex plots for the newly independent reader
- emphasis on reading for meaning

LEVEL 2

Library of Congress Cataloging-in-Publication Data Available

2 4 6 8 10 9 7 5 3 1

Published by Sterling Publishing Co., Inc.
387 Park Avenue South, New York, NY 10016
Text copyright © 2005 by Harriet Ziefert Inc.
Illustrations copyright © 2005 by Amanda Haley
Distributed in Canada by Sterling Publishing
c/o Canadian Manda Group, 165 Dufferin Street
Toronto, Ontario, Canada M6K 3H6
Distributed in Great Britain and Europe by Chris Lloyd at Orca Book
Services, Stanley House, Fleets Lane, Poole BH15 3AJ, England
Distributed in Australia by Capricorn Link (Australia) Pty. Ltd.
P.O. Box 704, Windsor, NSW 2756, Australia

I'm Going To Read is a trademark of Sterling Publishing Co., Inc.

Printed in China
All rights reserved

Sterling ISBN 1-4027-2718-6

Ready, Alice?

Pictures by Amanda Haley

Sterling Publishing Co., Inc.
New York

"Time to get up, Alice,"
said her mother.

"Not yet," said Alice.

"Time to get dressed, Alice,"
said her mother.

"Not yet," said Alice.

Alice got dressed.

She put on her shirt . . .

her jeans . . .

her socks . . .

and her shoes.

"Time for breakfast, Alice."

"Not yet," said Alice.

It looked like a nice day.

So Alice went downstairs.

"Good morning, Alice."

"Good morning, Alice,"
said her father.

"Ready for breakfast, Alice?"

Alice drank her juice
and took six bites of toast.

"Don't want my egg, Mom,"
said Alice.

"Eat it up," said Mom.
"You'll be hungry later."

Alice hit the top of her egg
with her fork.

"Careful, Alice!" said her mother.
"What a mess!" said her father.

Alice went upstairs.

She washed her
hands and face.

"Are you ready, Alice?"
called her mother.

"Well, we're waiting,"
said Dad. "Waiting to take
you to the beach."

Alice took off her shoes
and put on her sandals.

She took off her jeans
and put on her shorts.

Alice found her sun hat . . .

her pail and shovel . . .

hat   water   boat   pistol   net

her boat . . .

her water pistol . . .

and her net.

"Alice, we're ready to go!"
shouted her father.

Alice put on her sun hat.